CARTER HIGH
CHRONICLES

IT IS
Not a Date

By Eleanor Robins

SADDLEBACK
EDUCATIONAL PUBLISHING

CARTER HIGH
CHRONICLES

EDUCATIONAL PUBLISHING
www.sdlback.com

ISBN-13: 978-1-61651-309-2
ISBN-10: 1-61651-309-8
eBook: 978-1-60291-957-0

Printed in Guangzhou, China
0312/CA21200390

16 15 14 13 12   2 3 4 5 6 7

Chapter 1

It was Saturday morning. Kirk got his tennis racket. He went in the den. His mom and Beth were there. Beth was his sister. She was eight years old.

Kirk said, "I'm going to the park to play tennis."

Kirk was on the tennis team last year. He hoped to be on the tennis team this year too.

Beth ran up to him. She said, "Take me with you, Kirk."

"No way," Kirk said.

Beth yelled, "Make him take me, Mama. Make him take me."

"Stop yelling, Beth," his mom said.

Kirk hurried to the door. He knew Dan was waiting for him on the sidewalk. Dan was his best friend.

Kirk went outside.

He and Dan started to walk down the sidewalk.

Dan said, "What are you doing this afternoon? Are you going to work at the plant store?"

"Yeah," Kirk said.

Kirk worked there some on the weekends. He liked his job. He helped people find where plants were. Sometimes he took the plants to their cars.

He worked for Mr. Hill. Mr. Hill was the owner of the store.

Kirk said, "What are your plans for today?"

"I told Dad I would help him with some yard work. Tonight I have a date with Eve," Dan said.

Eve was Dan's girlfriend. They had been dating for almost a year.

"Where are you going?" Kirk asked.

"I don't know yet. It is Eve's turn to say where we go. She is still thinking about it. Her little sister is in the band. So I think she will say the band concert," Dan said.

"That sounds like fun," Kirk said.

Dan said, "I hope it will be. Where are you and Claire going?"

Claire was Kirk's girlfriend. They had been dating for four months.

"To a movie," Kirk said.

"Which one?" Dan asked.

"Some movie Claire wants to see. I forgot the name of it," Kirk said.

Dan said, "Let me know how you like the movie. Eve and I might want to see it next week."

"OK," Kirk said.

The guys got to the park.

They did some stretching exercises. Then Dan said, "Do you want to play some games? Or just hit the ball back and forth?"

"Play some games," Kirk said.

The guys played for a while.

Kirk won the first game. He was about to win the second game. But he hit the ball into the net. He went to the net to get the ball. Dan went to the net too.

Dan said, "A girl is watching us play. Do you know her?"

Kirk got the ball. Then he turned and looked at the girl.

"No, I don't. I have never seen her before. Have you?" Kirk said.

"She goes to our school. I've seen her in the hall. But she isn't in any of my classes," Dan said.

The girl left when she saw the boys were looking at her.

The boys played three games. Kirk won two of them.

Then Kirk said, "We had better stop now. I need to get home and eat lunch. I don't want to be late to work."

The boys started to walk back to Kirk's house.

Kirk said, "Do you want to do something Sunday afternoon?"

Dan said, "I can't. I have to study for a test. Be glad your teachers don't give Monday tests."

"Then I guess we won't talk again until Monday," Kirk said.

Chapter 2

Kirk ate lunch. Then he went to the plant store. He stayed busy the whole afternoon.

It was almost time for the store to close.

Mr. Hill said, "It's almost time to close, Kirk. Get those plants in front of the store. And bring them inside."

"OK," Kirk said.

Kirk started to the door.

A girl came in. She was the girl from the park. Kirk was surprised to see her.

The girl looked surprised to see Kirk.

A man was with her. They went over to Mr. Hill.

Kirk went outside to get the plants. He took all of the plants inside.

The man talked to Mr. Hill. But the girl kept looking at Kirk.

Mr. Hill said, "Kirk, time to close. Lock the door. And then come over here."

Kirk locked the door. He went over to Mr. Hill.

Mr. Hill said, "I want you to meet my brother. And my niece, Gail."

Kirk said, "Hi. Nice to meet you."

Gail smiled. She said, "You are a very good tennis player."

Mr. Hill said, "I didn't know you two knew each other."

Gail said, "We don't. I saw Kirk playing tennis at the park this morning."

Mr. Hill said, "Kirk is on the school tennis team. He is the best player on the team."

"That's great," Gail said.

Her dad said, "Gail hopes to be on the tennis team. She can hardly wait for the team try-outs next spring."

"Were you on the team at your other school?" Kirk asked.

Gail said, "No. I couldn't make the team last year. I needed to serve better to be on the team."

Her dad said, "Gail worked on her serves all summer. She serves a lot better now."

Gail said, "I do serve better. But not that much better."

Gail kept looking at Kirk. Did she want him to ask her for a tennis date? She seemed nice. And she was pretty. But he dated Claire. And they dated only each other.

Mr. Hill said, "Maybe Kirk could help you. Do you think you could, Kirk?"

How could Kirk say no? He had

needed a job last summer. Mr. Hill had given him a job. And now Mr. Hill let him work some on the weekends.

"Sure," Kirk said.

What else could he say?

Gail said, "I know you are busy. Do you really have time to help me?"

"Sure he does," Mr. Hill said. Then he looked over at Kirk.

"I have time," Kirk said.

What else could he say?

Gail smiled at Kirk. She said, "When can you help me? Any time is OK with me."

Kirk didn't know what to say. But Mr. Hill, Gail, and her dad were all looking at him.

"I don't know. I help with the football team after school. And I work here on Saturday afternoons," Kirk said.

Gail didn't say anything.

Mr. Hill said, "What about next

Saturday morning? Would that be OK?"

"Sure," Kirk said.

What else could he say?

Gail said, "Great. I could meet you at the park about 9:00."

"Sure. Fine," Kirk said.

But he didn't really feel that way.

"Good. It is a date," Mr. Hill said.

A date?

Kirk didn't know what to say. He didn't think it was a date. It was only a tennis lesson. Not a date. He hoped Gail didn't think it was a date.

"See you Saturday," Gail said.

Then she and her dad left.

Mr. Hill said, "Thanks, Kirk. It's very nice of you to help Gail."

How could he not help her?

Mr. Hill had been very nice to him. He couldn't say he wouldn't help Mr. Hill's niece.

But what would Claire say when she found out?

He was sure it would be OK with Claire. He would only be helping a girl with her tennis.

Claire was nice. She wouldn't get mad about that.

Or would she?

Chapter 3

Kirk wanted to talk to Dan. He called Dan as soon as he got home.

Dan said, "I didn't think you would call today."

"I wasn't going to call. But I need to talk to you about something," Kirk said.

"What?" Dan asked.

"The girl we saw at the park is Mr. Hill's niece. Her name is Gail. I might have a date with her," Kirk said.

"You might have a date with her? Did I hear you right?" Dan asked.

"You did," Kirk said. "I thought you and Claire dated only each other," Dan said.

Kirk said, "We do."

"Then why did you ask Gail for a date?" Dan asked.

Kirk said, "I didn't. And I don't think it is a date. That's why I called you. I want to know what you think."

"Why do you need to know what I think? A date is a date. You have one. Or you don't. Which is it?" Dan said.

Kirk said, "She wants to be on the tennis team. She needs help with her serves. Mr. Hill asked me to help her."

"And you said you would," Dan said.

"Mr. Hill has been nice to me. I had to say I would. It's only a tennis lesson. Not a date. But Mr. Hill said it is a date."

"When did you say you would help her? After school?" Dan asked.

Kirk said, "No. Next Saturday morning."

"Claire is going to be very mad at you," Dan said.

Kirk said, "Why? It is not a date. It's only a tennis lesson."

Dan laughed. Then he said, "That's what you think. It sounds like a date to me. And Claire will think it is too."

Kirk said, "Claire is nice. She will not get mad. She will say it is OK to help Gail."

Dan said, "Claire is nice. But we are talking about you playing tennis with a girl. Would you want Claire to give a guy a tennis lesson?"

"No," Kirk said. He wouldn't like that at all.

Dan laughed. He said, "I thought you would say that."

"But it isn't the same thing," Kirk said.

"Why isn't it?" Dan said.

Kirk said, "I would know the guy was wanting to date Claire. And that Claire might want to date him."

"Then you know how Claire might feel," Dan said.

Dan was right. Claire might not like it. She might think he wanted to date Gail.

"Maybe I shouldn't tell Claire. She will be out of town next weekend. So I won't have to tell her. She won't be here. So she won't know about the tennis lesson," Kirk said.

Dan said, "You better tell Claire. Before she hears about it from someone else."

"I don't plan to tell Claire. And you won't tell her. So how will she find out?" Kirk said.

Dan said, "Gail goes to our school. She could tell someone Claire knows.

Or someone could see you at the park. Marge might find out. And she would tell the whole school."

Marge was in some of their classes. She was always talking about people. And saying things about them that weren't always true.

Kirk said, "You're right. I forgot you said Gail went to our school. I should tell Claire. I just hope she doesn't get mad."

But he had a feeling she would.

Kirk had to hurry and get ready for his date with Claire. He should not have talked so long to Dan.

His mom called him to come and eat. His mom and little sister Beth were already at the table.

Kirk sat down.

His mom said, "Are you going somewhere with Dan? Or do you have a date with Claire?"

"Claire and I are going to a movie," Kirk said.

Beth said, "I want to go too. Will you take me with you?"

"No," Kirk said.

"Make him take me, Mama. Make him take me, Mama," Beth said.

"Be quiet and eat, Beth," his mom said.

"Please take me, Kirk," Beth said.

Kirk said, "No way will I take you. It would not be a date with you along."

Chapter 4

Kirk ate quickly. He was in a hurry to get to Claire's house. He didn't want to be late.

Kirk went to Claire's house. He rang the doorbell.

Claire quickly opened the door. She was ready to go.

Kirk said, "We have some time before we need to go. OK for me to come in?"

"Sure," Claire said.

Kirk went in the house. He and Claire sat down on the sofa.

Kirk didn't want to tell Claire about Gail. But Dan was right. He had better do it. He might as well tell her now. And not have to worry about it during the show.

"I need to tell you something," Kirk said.

"What?" Claire said.

"I met Mr. Hill's niece today at the store with her dad," Kirk said.

Kirk stopped talking. He wasn't sure how to tell Claire about the tennis lesson.

"And?" Claire asked.

"Mr. Hill asked me to help her with tennis. And I said I would," Kirk said.

"Why does he want you to help her?" Claire asked.

"She wants to be on the tennis team. And she needs to learn to serve better," Kirk said.

"Where are you planning to help her? At school?" Claire asked.

Kirk said, "No. At the park. Next

Saturday morning. I said I would meet her there."

Claire quickly got up from the sofa. She said, "Date that girl. And you can forget about me."

Kirk got up. He said, "You're wrong, Claire. It is a tennis lesson. Not a date. Mr. Hill asked me to help Gail with her tennis."

"And you have to do it because he asked you?" Claire said.

Kirk said, "Yes. Mr. Hill has been very nice to me. And I told you. It is not a date."

"I don't care what you call it. You're meeting a girl to play tennis. That is a date," Claire said.

"You could go with us. But you won't be here," Kirk said.

"And you knew that when you made the date," Claire said.

"I told you. It is not a date," Kirk said.

"And I told you it was," Claire said.

Kirk thought they should stop talking about it. The sooner they got to the movie the better.

He said, "We need to go. Or we will be late to the movie."

"Are you going to break your date with that girl?" Claire asked.

Kirk said, "I told you. It is not a date. And I have to help Gail. I told Mr. Hill I would. He is counting on me. So I have to help her."

"No, you don't. And I am not going to the movie with you. You can just forget about our date. And you can just go," Claire said.

"Why?" Kirk asked.

"No way am I going to date you again. Unless you break your date with that girl," Claire said.

"It is not a date," Kirk said.

"Stop saying that. Because it is a date," Claire said.

Kirk knew he might as well go.

He didn't want to stop dating Claire. But he had to help Gail with her tennis.

What was he going to do?

Chapter 5

Kirk left Claire's house. He wanted to go see Dan. But he knew Dan had a date.

He could go to a movie. But he didn't want to go by himself. The movie wouldn't be any fun without Claire. And he didn't want anyone to ask why Claire wasn't with him.

He went home.

His mom looked surprised to see him. She said, "Why are you home so soon, Kirk? Is something wrong?"

"Claire wouldn't go out with me," Kirk said.

His mom looked even more surprised. She said, "Why?"

Kirk said, "I met Mr. Hill's niece today. Her name is Gail. Mr. Hill asked me to help Gail with her tennis. I said I would. And Claire got mad at me."

"Why?" his mom asked.

"I said I would meet Gail at the park. Next Saturday morning. Claire thinks it is a date. But it isn't. It is only a tennis lesson," Kirk said.

"Did you tell Claire it wasn't a date?" his mom asked.

"Yes. But she still said it was," Kirk said.

"Take Claire with you," his mom said.

Kirk said, "I can't. She will be out of town."

"I think it's nice you're going to help Mr. Hill's niece. Don't worry about

Claire. She will get over it. Just give her some time," his mom said.

Kirk knew Claire better than his mom did. He knew Claire wouldn't get over it. Unless he told Gail he couldn't help her.

Kirk said, "She won't get over it, Mom. Unless I tell Gail I can't help her."

His mom said, "Are you going to do that?"

How could he do that? He didn't want to let Mr. Hill down. He didn't want to hurt Gail's feelings, either.

But he liked Claire a lot. And he didn't want to stop dating her.

How could he get Claire to say it was OK to help Gail?

Kirk said, "I don't know what to do. I don't want Claire to break up with me. But I don't want to tell Mr. Hill that

I can't help Gail. What do you think I should do?"

His mom said, "I am not going to tell you what to do. It is up to you. You have to do what you think is best."

But Kirk didn't know what was best. He just knew he wanted to keep dating Claire.

Chapter 6

Kirk called Claire on Sunday. But she would not talk to him. He wanted to call Dan. But he knew Dan had to study for a test.

He didn't get to talk to Dan until Monday. He didn't see Dan until they went to lunch.

They quickly got their lunch trays. They went over to a table and sat down.

Dan said, "What movie did you and Claire go to see?"

"We didn't go to the movie," Kirk said.

"I thought Claire wanted to see a movie," Dan said.

"She did," Kirk said.

"So why didn't you go?" Dan asked.

"Claire wouldn't go out with me. And she told me to leave," Kirk said.

Dan looked very surprised. He said, "Why?"

"I told her about Mr. Hill's niece. And she got mad at me," Kirk said.

"What did she say?" Dan asked.

"She said it was a date. She said she wouldn't date me again. Unless I broke my date with Mr. Hill's niece. I told her it was only a tennis lesson. But she still said it was a date," Kirk said.

"What are you going to do?" Dan asked.

"I don't know," Kirk said.

"You can back out of helping Mr. Hill's niece," Dan said.

"But I don't know how I can do that," Kirk said.

"Do you think he would fire you?" Dan said.

Kirk said, "No. But he has been nice to me. And I don't want to let him down."

"Maybe Claire will change her mind. Do you think she will?" Dan said.

"No," Kirk said.

"You might have to get a new girl-friend," Dan said.

"I don't want a new girlfriend," Kirk said.

"Have you called Claire since Saturday night?" Dan asked.

"I called her yesterday. But she wouldn't talk to me," Kirk said.

"Have you seen her today?" Dan asked.

Kirk said, "No. I looked for her. I didn't see her. But I'm sure she is at school."

"Call her after practice. Maybe she isn't mad at you now. And maybe she will talk to you," Dan said.

Kirk hoped Claire wasn't still mad at him. But he thought she would be.

Kirk ate his lunch. Then he said, "See you after school, Dan."

Kirk left the lunch room and started to class. He saw Claire. She was walking down the hall in front of him.

He called to her. He said, "Wait, Claire. I'll walk with you."

Claire started to walk very fast. She acted like she didn't hear him.

But Kirk knew she did hear him.

Kirk started to go after her. But Marge got in his way.

Marge said, "Is something wrong, Kirk? Is Claire mad at you? Have the two of you broken up? I heard you ask her to wait. But she didn't."

Claire is not mad at me. And we have

not broken up," Kirk said too quickly.

"Then why didn't she wait for you?" Marge asked.

"She was just in a hurry. And she didn't hear me," Kirk said.

He hoped Marge believed him. He didn't want her to tell people that Claire was mad at him. And that they had broken up.

Kirk said, "I have to go. I have to get to class."

He wanted to go after Claire. But it was too late for him to catch up with her.

Chapter 7

The week seemed very long to Kirk. He kept trying to talk to Claire. But she would not talk to him.

He thought a lot about what he should do.

Football practice didn't last long on Thursday. So Kirk went to the plant store. He was going to tell Mr. Hill about Claire. And that she didn't want him to help Gail. Maybe Mr. Hill would say it was OK not to help Gail.

Mr. Hill looked surprised to see him. He said, "Hi, Kirk. I thought you had practice today."

Kirk said, "I did. But the team didn't practice as long today. Do you need any help?"

"I sure do. I just got in a truck full of plants. You can help me unload them. Then I'll tell you where to put them."

Kirk started to unload the truck.

He worked hard. He got all the plants unloaded. Then he walked over to Mr. Hill.

Kirk said, "I got all the plants unloaded. Where do you want them?"

Mr. Hill said, "Good work, Kirk. I didn't think you would get the truck unloaded that fast."

He told Kirk where to put the plants.

Then Kirk said, "I need to talk to you. Do you have time to talk now?"

A man came in the store.

Mr. Hill said, "Not now, Kirk. I need to help this man first."

Mr. Hill went to help the man. Kirk started to put the plants up.

The man bought some plants. Then he left.

Mr. Hill walked over to Kirk. He said, "Thank you for coming to help today, Kirk. And thank you for saying you will help Gail. It means a lot to me. I know how busy you are."

Kirk didn't say anything.

Mr. Hill said, "What did you want to talk to me about?"

Kirk still wanted to tell Mr. Hill that he couldn't help Gail. But how could he tell him now?

Maybe he should call Gail. He could tell her about Claire. Then Gail would know he had a girlfriend. Maybe she wouldn't want him to help her then.

Kirk said, "Can you give me Gail's phone number? I may need to call her."

Mr. Hill said, "Sure. I should have already given it to you."

He quickly wrote down the number for Kirk. Then he gave it to Kirk.

"Thanks," Kirk said.

Kirk didn't want to tell Mr. Hill he couldn't help Gail. And he wasn't sure he should call Gail.

Would she say it was OK not to help her?

Or would she be upset?

Chapter 8

Gail and her dad came in the store.

Kirk was surprised to see them. He didn't know they would be there.

They walked over to Mr. Hill and Kirk.

Gail smiled at Kirk. She said, "Hi, Kirk. I didn't know you would be here."

"Hi," Kirk said.

Mr. Hill looked at his brother. He said, "I'm glad you came by. The plants you wanted came today. I put them in a box for you. I was going to call you tonight."

The two men walked to the back of the store.

Maybe it was good Gail and her dad came to the store. Maybe it was better to tell her about Claire now. And not tell her on the phone.

But Gail spoke before Kirk could.

She said, "You are so nice to help me. I know I will play tennis better after you do. Maybe I will play a lot better. And be able to make the tennis team."

How could Kirk say that he wouldn't help her?

"See you Saturday," Gail said.

"Sure. See you Saturday," Kirk said.

Gail went over to Mr. Hill and her dad.

Kirk put the rest of the plants up. Then he left the store and went home.

He called Claire as soon as he got home. But she wouldn't talk to him.

He did some homework. Then his mom called him to eat.

His mom said, "Did you work everything out with Claire?"

Kirk said, "No. I called her when I got home. She still won't talk to me."

Kirk ate. Then he went in the den to watch TV. He was trying to get his mind off of Claire. But it didn't help to watch TV.

His sister Beth got between him and the TV. She had a game in her hand. She said, "Play a game with me, Kirk."

"Go away, Beth," Kirk said.

His mom said, "Be nice to your sister, Kirk."

"Mama, make Kirk play this game with me. Make him, Mama," Beth said.

Kirk said, "I'm going to my room. I need to study some more."

He got up and went to his room. He did study some. But most of the time he thought about Claire.

What was he going to do? He didn't want to stop dating Claire. He wanted to work things out with her. But how?

His tennis lesson with Gail was not a date. But how could he get Claire to see it that way?

His mom came to the door. She said, "Are you OK, Kirk?"

"Yeah," Kirk said. But he didn't feel OK.

"Did you get all of your studying done?" his mom asked.

"All that I need to do tonight," Kirk said.

His mom said, "Beth thinks you are mad at her."

"Tell her that I'm not mad at her. I am just upset about Claire," Kirk said.

His mom said, "Why don't you come play a game with Beth? Then she will know you are not mad at her.

And it might help you get your mind off of Claire."

Kirk didn't want to play a game with Beth. But he said, "OK. I will be in there in a few minutes."

Kirk stayed in his room a few more minutes. Then he got up to go to the den.

On his way to the den he got an idea. Why didn't he think of it sooner?

He could take Beth with him to the park. Then Claire would know it was not a date.

Kirk hurried into the den. He said, "Beth, I'm going to the park Saturday. I'm going to help a girl with her tennis. Do you want to go with me? You can chase the tennis balls for us."

Beth started to jump up and down. She looked very happy. She said, "Oh, yes, yes. That will be so much fun."

Kirk didn't think it was fun to chase

tennis balls. But he was glad Beth thought it would be.

Kirk said, "And I will play a game with you now. But first I have to call Claire."

Kirk hurried to the phone. He called Claire.

Claire answered.

Kirk started to talk as fast as he could. He didn't want Claire to hang up before he told her about Beth.

"Beth is going to the park with me Saturday. So it won't be just Gail and me. Beth will be with us," he said.

"You are going to take Beth with you?" Claire said. She sounded very surprised.

Kirk said, "Yes. She will chase the tennis balls. Now you can't say it will be a date. I wouldn't take Beth with me on a date."

Claire didn't say anything. But she did not hang up.

"You know it will not be a date, Claire. Not with Beth there. You know how she is," Kirk said.

"I sure do," Claire said. Then she laughed.

That made Kirk feel a lot better. He knew Claire wasn't mad at him any more.

Kirk said, "I will call you Sunday. Maybe you will get back home early. And we can go somewhere."

Claire said, "OK. But be sure you take Beth to the park with you."

"I will," Kirk said.

"I have to go now. Be sure you call me Sunday," Claire said.

"I will," Kirk said.

Claire wasn't mad at him anymore. So he could help Gail with her tennis. And he could still have Claire for a girlfriend.